WHEN
WINDWAGON SMITH CAME TO WESTPORT

· WHEN ·
WINDWAGON SMITH
CAME TO WESTPORT

RAMONA MAHER

LAVISHLY ILLUSTRATED BY TOM ALLEN

COWARD, McCANN & GEOGHEGAN, INC.
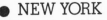
NEW YORK

Text copyright © 1977 by Ramona Maher
Illustrations copyright © 1977 by Tom Allen   All rights reserved.
This book, or parts thereof, may not be reproduced
in any form without permission in writing from the publishers.
Published simultaneously in Canada by Longman Canada Limited.
SBN: TR—698-20407-7

Library of Congress Cataloging in Publication Data
Maher, Ramona. When Windwagon Smith came to Westport.
Summary: Windwagon Smith tries to persuade the people of Westport
to replace slow ox-drawn wagons with a flotilla of wind-powered wagons.
(1. Folklore—United States) I. Allen, Tom. II. Title.
PZ8.1.W44Wh 813'.5'4 (398.2) 77-442

Printed in the United States of America

First, the bluetick hound barked.

It was a summer day in 1853, with a hot breeze blowing
just enough to keep the skeeters off
and just enough
to stir around
the smells of vinegar, tar soap, and coffee
in our store—
called Ericssen's Emporium.

The dog began to yelp.

Up till then it was a plain kind of day.
I'd been weighing nails.
Pa was stacking soda crackers.
Ma wrapped up bolts of calico cloth.

Then the hound scooted in,
tail between its legs.

"Shoo!" said Ma.
She flapped her apron.
"Who left that door open? Did you, Eric?"
The dog whined.
He hid behind a bag of wheat.
Then two chickens clucked in.
"Great day!" cried Mother.
She whisked around the counter.
"What's going on?
Out, you feathered varmints!"
She clapped her hands at the chickens.
"Pigs will come next, I suppose."
Ma grabbed a broom.

Pa began to laugh and got off his stepladder.
The chickens squawked two times around the flour barrel.
Ma's broom went *swoosh!*
The chickens cackled out the door again
in a cloud of feathers, spilled flour, and sawdust.
I slipped out soon as Ma's back was turned.
The horses tied to the hitching post
reared and kicked up dust.

Two Pawnee Indians raced down the main street
on their paint ponies.

A mile away, you could hear the Winter twins yelling.
Then four coyotes yelped past,
trying to outrun whatever it was that was coming.

Miz Yoakum came puffing out of her house.
Her face was red.
Her sunbonnet hung by its strings, half on and half off.
"Is it redskins?" she hollered.
Then she fell over like a blob of jelly.
Miz Yoakum fainted
right in front of our store!

Mr. Newsom, the Indian agent, and his assistant
craned their heads out of their second story office
above the jail.
"What's causing all the dust?" called Mr. Newsom.

The Winter twins tore up, lickety split,
breathless and pointing.
"It's a wagon, but it's no Conestoga!" said Jack Winter.
Even from this distance you could see
the top wasn't Conestoga round.
"It's a wagon, but it's not a Yankee spring wagon,"
echoed Jill Winter.
"A Yankee wagon would have a square top."

"If it's a wagon, what's pulling the darned thing?
There's no horse," I said.

"Must be
a ball of cotton
come to call,"
cackled Walleyed Jake
from behind the swinging doors
of the Possum Kingdom Saloon.

All around people were staring down the road,
straining to get a look at the contraption.
It came zigging to the right,
past cottonwoods and hostelries.
It went zagging to the left,
past livestock pens and wagon yards.
It was getting closer.
"It's a ship!" I said to the twins
and to the Reverend Winter.
The thing looked like pictures I'd seen of ships.

Pa came out to join the crowd.
He took off his storekeeper's apron
and cleaned his specs.
"I don't know what you'd call it," he said.
"It has a white sail like a ship," I said.
"And wheels like a wagon," chanted the Winter twins.

Mr. Sager moseyed up.
He owned Sager's Wagon Yard.
"Looks like a wagon rolling backward,
with wind in a sail for power," said Mr. Sager.
Now we could see
a small man standing in the wagon.
His hand was on the wagon tongue.
"He's using the tongue like a tiller, to steer with," stated Pa.
The sail bellied in a sudden gust
and the ship or wagon zigzagged a little faster.
Walleyed Jake and two other men hunkered down
by the Possum Kingdom Saloon
to watch the thing and its driver draw nearer.

The driver was tanned the color
of an old leather boot.
He wore an old blue suit with gold braid.
One gold earring stuck out from his blue hat.
It made him look lopsided.
Like a seafaring man,
I thought.

The man pulled a rope
and the sail dropped.
As the wind puffed out of the dropped sail,
the wagon rolled to a standstill
in front of Ericssen's Emporium—our store!
The little man
wrapped the canvas sail around the boom.
He tied it with a strip of hemp.

Miz Yoakum forgot about her faint.
"Well, I never saw the like!"
She laughed and got up.

The newspaper owner, Mr. Orpheus, crossed the street.

The stranger set the wagon brake.
He threw a brass anchor to the ground.
He whacked dust from his blue hat.
He tossed a rope ladder over the side,
climbed down to dry land,
and bowed to Miz Yoakum and to Ma.
Then he waved his hat to the rest of us.

"Where am I, young tar?" he asked me.
"Why—you're in Westport, Missouri," I told him.
Westport is the town
where most wagon trains set out for Santa Fe
to trade with Mexico.
That's why
there's so many wagon yards and outfitters here.

When we first came to Westport,
Pa explained it wasn't for keeps.
He planned that we'd fit out the wagon trains,
sell them supplies and such.
We'd become rich and buy a ship
and become sailors on a real sea.

After a year or two, though,
Pa stopped talking about buying a ship.
I wondered if he'd forgotten.
I hadn't.
I walked to the windwagon
and looked over the sides.
A compass was tied to the tongue or tiller.
A compass face is round, like a clock,
and has a needle that always points true north.
"Welcome to Windwagon One," the driver shouted.
I looked up.
High on the mast was a crow's nest—
the place where a sailor stands
to look for whales and other ships.
Why would he need
a crow's nest in the middle of a prairie,
I wondered.

Then he said,
"I'm Windwagon Smith out of Nickport, Massachusetts.
A single gentleman
under the influence of wind and stars.
Who might you be, mate?"
"I'm Eric Ericssen," I answered.
"A sailor's name, sure as I'm a sailor," boomed the stranger.

He slapped me on the shoulder and turned to
all the people who'd lined up on the board sidewalks
to gawk at him and his wagon.
"They call me Windwagon Smith, Captain of the Plains."
He strutted a bit; his feet seemed to plant themselves
on the deck of a pitching ship as he walked.

"I plan to build a fleet of windships
to carry trade goods to Santa Fe.
In this little windwagon here,
I can sail there fast and true.
The Santa Fe Trail is 770 miles long,
the way an ox wagon travels.
That ox wagon takes two months.
The way I go,
as the crow flies,
I skim over the sand hills
and through buffalo wallows.
I bypass sandbars and whirl over quicksand.
The wind sails me right along.
I don't worry about carrying food or water
for oxen or mules or horses.
I just light out across the plains in Windwagon One.
I make it to Santa Fe in two weeks.
I figure a *big* wagon, loaded with supplies,
could sail there in three or four days!"
"What if the wind blows easterly
when you want to go west?"
asked the baker, Mr. Fennel.

"I drop anchor, my hearty.
I wait until the wind rises to sail me west again,"
replied Windwagon Smith.
"Now, I have a business proposition.
First, I'll wet my whistle.
Then I'll want to talk to the banker."

I watched the windwagon until Mr. Smith came back
from the saloon, the newspaper, and the bank.
"What's a captain doing inland
so far from the ocean?" I asked.

"Look again," said the small brown man.
"Outside this fair city, I see
long, emerald swells—
just like the ocean.
I see wide level stretches like floating kelp.
I see white topped flowers
that are like whitecapped waves.
Bless me, Eric,
I've sat through the dripping doldrums off Hong Kong
and storms off Siberia!
I've been in a clipper ship
on wide, smooth water.
You couldn't tell the difference between that ocean
and this sea of grass.
You live near a sea, I tell ye, laddie!"
I tell you truly, lad,
Westport is a port town!"

I'd watched the grass curl and dip and rise.
By the great horned spoon,
it did look like pictures of the ocean, I thought.

Miz Yoakum rented Windwagon a room
while he tried to set up his windwagon company.
He walked with his rolling gait about Westport,
wearing his uniform
and carrying plans and lists of figures.
Some days he told me tales of the sea.
One time, while mending his tack,
Captain Windwagon Smith
told me about his tattoo.
The tattoo was a big blue rock
inked on his upper arm.
A green mermaid perched on the rock.
"Had it done
on a three-ply junk on the China Seas," he said.
"Oh, I was a fine lad for the rigging loft and spars,
up there with the gulls
over the open sea, Eric Ericssen."

"No gulls here," I told him.
"But you've got eagles and hawks
and quail and grouse.
Those are proud prairie gulls,"
said Windwagon.
"And talk about your schools of cod and dolphin!
There are schools of buffalo
and deer and elk out here!

Windwagon Smith's stories
made me see things in a way
I'd never seen them before.
But Windwagon's plan for a fleet of windships
seemed to be coming to nothing.
The bankers and traders of Westport hooted.
"Whoever heard of a dryland navy?" they asked
when he tried to raise money
for the first cargo wagon in a whole fleet
of Santa Fe Trail windships.
Even Walleyed Jake and the bartender
started saying
that Windwagon Smith had
barnacles on his brain.

"Very well," said Windwagon,
when Banker Adams turned him down
the third time.
"I'll take my plans and my blueprints for the fleet
to the good people of Council Grove."
He moistened a finger and tested the breeze.
He bought tar and tallow and greased an axle.
He raised the sail on his tiny wagon.
Mr. Sager snorted with laughter as nothing happened.
Then the white sheet caught the breeze.
The wagon started down the road
like a hawk with widespread wings.
The windwagon worked all right!
What if a big windship *could* cover
all those miles to Santa Fe
in three weeks instead of two months?
They'd be rich.
You could almost hear the Westport merchants thinking.

"Wait!" shouted the mayor.
"Let us think this over one more time!"
called Mr. Orpheus,
the newspaper owner.
"We'll study your plan some more!" cried Banker Adams.
"It *might* work," said my Pa to Mr. Sager.

"We don't want Council Grove to get hold of a good idea.
A good idea we let sail past under our noses."
That's what Mr. Adams said to Mr. Orpheus.
"Tell Mr. Smith
we've reconsidered, Eric," Banker Adams said to me.

I took off, running as fast as I could.
Luckily, Windwagon Smith saw me
and yanked on the brake.
I helped him pull the light wagon against the wind—
back to the bank.
Banker Adams clapped Windwagon on the shoulder.
Everybody crowded around papers and plans
spread out on the marble counter in the bank.

That's how the people of Westport and Windwagon Smith
started the Overland Navigation Company.

We held a catfish and chicken fry.
Everybody came and ate like pigs in a cornfield.
Windwagon Smith told again his dream
of a fleet of windships.
He unrolled his blueprints
and talked about cargo space in the holds.
He talked about using water in kegs for ballast.
"They'll keep the weight even as we speed along," he said.
Then he sang us a song about Captain Kidd.

The first windship that would carry cargo to Santa Fe
took two months to build.
Hickory wood was brought
downriver from St. Louis for the decks.
Steel for some of the fittings came from Pittsburgh.
Instead of using a wagon tongue for a tiller,
we attached a real helm to a fancy gearbox.

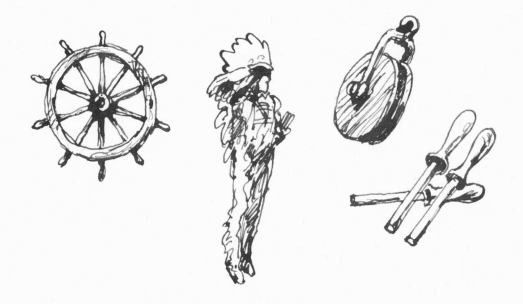

The wagon was twenty-five feet, end to end.
She was seven feet deep below decks
and seven feet across her beam.
The wheels were twelve feet across.
The mast was painted blue.
The figurehead was a cigar store Indian,
colored red, white, and blue.
I got to holystone the deck.
That means I polished it
with something called rotten stone
until the wood was smooth as water.
Then I waxed it with beeswax.

The whole town came
to watch Windwagon launch the big ship.
Overland Number One, it was called.

Ladies wore hoopskirts that ballooned in the breeze.

The Winter twins
stood in the goldenrod
and sneezed a lot.

Our Senator wore a top hat.

Four men climbed the gangplank to be on board
with Captain Smith for the first voyage.
They were the main stockholders—Lawyer Mastin,
Mr. Orpheus,
Banker Adams, and Mr. Newsom.
And me, I was aboard too.
I hid in a cupboard below decks.
"You don't
own stock in the company, Eric," said Windwagon
when I told him I wanted to come along.
"But I've worked
harder than any of them!" I protested.
I was proud of the prairie ship.
I wanted to go on her maiden voyage.

Windwagon tugged his one gold earring.
"If you were to hide below decks
in the supply cupboard,
no one would know," he mused.
"You can look out the porthole.
Hold onto these metal rings
and sit on this coil of rope."
I did as he told me.
Soon the wagon began to move.
Two yoke of oxen pulled Overland Number One
to the plains west of town.
The grass tops were big green waves.
I heard Mr. Newsom laugh.
Lawyer Mastin danced a hornpipe.
I heard his Santa Fe boots clog up and down
on the hickory deck.
"Careful of those polished boards!"
I wanted to tell him.

Banker Adams hoisted the anchor.
Windwagon ran the main sail up the mast.
"Sure the day's
not too windy for this?" asked Mr. Orpheus.
"Cast off!" shouted Windwagon Smith.

Those big wheels on the windship
floated over the prairie dog holes.
We tickled a ditch or two.
Soon the windship was rolling faster than ever!

I tried hard not to cough.
Dust was piling high as goosefeathers.
The water keg got loose
and rolled around below decks,
banging the cupboards.
I hung on hard to the metal rings.
Rocks flew up and hit the sides of the windship.

"Ain't she going too fast?" yelled Mr. Newsom.
"It is a mite fresh out today," said Windwagon Smith.
"Just pretend we're running before a storm!
See the waves part before us mates?"
I heard the sail snap
and the windship tacked to the right.
"Hold on, boys!" said our captain grandly.
"We'll ride out this storm."

"I think I'm going to be seasick," howled Lawyer Mastin.
"Be sick over the side, over the side, me hearty,"
ordered Windwagon Smith.

I was starting to feel fearful.
The sail was snapping
like a turtle in the Missouri River.
"Watch! I'll run against the wind!"
Windwagon put the helm over.
I did a flip-flop in my cupboard.
The big ship came about, sure enough.
All the timbers groaned, but the ship
seemed to be right side up.
So was I, I decided.

The ship kept bouncing.
"Something's wrong!" I heard Mr. Newsom shout.
"Turn around!"
"Can't.
The helm is stuck," hollered Captain Windwagon Smith.
"Mastin, stop being sick.
Help me unjam this gearbox."
"Oh-h," Mastin moaned.
"I feel like seven buffalo kicked me in the belly."
The wagon shivered and pitched.
The load seemed to shift.
My peephole showed we'd lost Lawyer Mastin
and his buffalo-sized bellyache.
"Man overboard!" piped Windwagon.
"Never mind. He's up and walking.
He's safe."

Around and around we sailed.
We swirled past Lawyer Mastin.
"I'll sue!" he cried.
"Why, this is smooth weather,"
Windwagon shouted
in the teeth of the wind.
"I could eat a bowl of whale soup
in a Cape Cod dory
and never spill a drop."
Through a crack in the boards,
I saw that Mr. Newsom
looked green.
I felt seasick myself.

We hailed and howdeyed to the east.
Then we skipped-to-my-Lou to the west.
The other three men dropped over the side
when the wagon made a slow bow to the north.

"Rats leaving the ship, be ye?"
bellowed our captain.
"Ye be nothing but horse and buggy men!
Chowderheads!"

I climbed up on the deck.
My head turned like a weathercock in the high wind.
Windwagon Smith grinned at me through ropes and lines.
He twirled the useless helm with one hand.
With the other, he pushed at the frozen gear.
"What ho, matey?"
The sea still seemed to be rough around me,
so I held on to an iron brace.

"Got your sea legs?"
Windwagon Smith laughed at his joke.
The windwagon dipped around that sea of grass,
making circles and loops and scrolls.
Then one of the big wheels sagged into a dry waterhole
on Turkey Creek.
The hole was so deep,
the wind couldn't pull us out.
The sail flapped. The sail kersnapped.
The wheels groaned like old men
as the wagon settled.
A spoke in the hub cracked.
Windwagon looked sadly at the chipped paint
and the broken wheel.
I helped him lower the sail.
He untied his compass from the helm.
We walked alone across the sea of grass
toward Westport.

"The gear could have stuck for anybody," I said,
to Captain Smith as we limped into town.
But the banker, the lawyer, the newspaper owner,
and the Indian agent shook their heads.
"We want nothing more to do with windwagons,
the Overland Navigation Company,
or with you,"
they said.
They banged the door in his face.
They even pulled down the shades
and latched the screen!
"Council Grove
won't have anything to do with you either!"
shouted Lawyer Mastin through a brass keyhole.
Windwagon yelled back through the keyhole,
"Cowards!
  I'll go elsewhere.
The world isn't full of shortsighted landcrabs
such as yourselves.
Praise Neptune!" he added.

"You should have run and hid
like the dogs and chickens, you—
you landlubbers!" I yelled,
taking my turn at the keyhole.

Captain Smith fetched his duffel bag
—his possible sack, he called it—
from the Widow Yoakum.
I trailed his rolling gait to the small wagon,
Windwagon One,
the vehicle he had come to Westport in.
It was behind our store, covered with canvas
to keep out dust.

"Let me come with you," I begged.
"I'll be a boy of all work.
I'll read the compass for you.
I'll clean the brass. Oil the wheels and pulleys.
Peel potatoes. Anything!
I'm not afraid!"

Windwagon laughed. "Bully for you, Eric.
I've sailed through Cape Horn storms,
Compared to them
today's little breeze was like two shakes
of a lamb's tail."
"You'll take me along then?" I asked.
Windwagon thought as he rigged the sail and
spliced the main brace.
"You stay here, Eric Ericssen,"
he answered at last.
"Go to school.
Study your numbers.
Learn about stars.
Read *Bowditch*.
Sailors must know those things." He winked.
"There be many seas in the world, young tar.
Those who stop at the edge of a sea
—be it a sea of water
or a sea of grass—never get anywhere.
Remember that, mate."

He gave me his compass as a farewell gift.
Then Windwagon Smith cast off.
I waved and waved.
At last, I couldn't see the white sail anymore.
It was lost between the blue sky
and the rippling grass on the plains.

People say they've seen Windwagon Smith.
A Mormon pack train said he led them to water
and cast off again.
Sioux Indians said that a wagon
and a small man in blue
passed them on the plains.
No horses, no mules pulled that wagon,
they swore to it.
The thing just rolled along
under a big white buffalo robe,
they said.

If you run across
a small brown man with a mermaid tattoo,
a man who rolls when he moves
like he is walking on a pitching deck,
that's Windwagon Smith.
I hope he still has
his blueprints for a fleet of windships.
I hope he still has his possible sack and his dreams.

Now, here I am—me, Eric Ericssen.
I am out of school.
I've learned about numbers.
I can sight by stars.
I'm ready as I'll ever be to sail the seas—
one of the seven seas of water
or a desert sea from the back of a camel
or the sea of grass right outside of Westport.

Maybe I'll set out for Santa Fe on my own.
Pa says that is fine with him,
and he tells Ma not to cry.
Those who stop at the edge of a sea—
be it a sea of water or a sea of grass—
never get anywhere.

Just as Captain Windwagon Smith said.

AUTHOR'S NOTE

In 1853 the frontier of the United States had shifted
from the Mississippi westward to the Pacific and
southward to the Rio Grande. Hunger for land,
adventure, and riches to be wrested from crops, new
products, gold, and furs sent farmers, tradesmen,
turnpikers, canalmen, and restless adolescents to the
West.

Many of the migrants congregated at Independence,
Missouri, or across the river, at Westport, to start
the 800-mile journey to Santa Fe. Santa Fe, New
Mexico Territory, was the northern point of trade
transactions with Mexico. The journeys were under-
taken in caravans of clumsy, ox-drawn wagons,
made clumsier by the food supplies carried. To
sustain each traveler, says Josiah Gregg, in his
exhaustive *The Commerce of the Prairies* (ed. Max L.
Moorhead; Norman, Okla., 1954), along went fifty
pounds of flour, fifty of bacon, ten of coffee, twenty
of sugar, plus stores of salt, beans, and crackers.

A faster means of travel was obviously required to cut
the logistics of trading with Mexico and the West
Coast.

Mechanically minded men—inventors, surveyors,
and estimators—started planning for railroads to
connect East and West; meanwhile, dreamers and
schemers came up with their own ideas of the most
rapid means of travel into the 850,000 square miles of
country acquired by the Treaty of Guadalupe Hidalgo
between the United States and Mexico. That treaty,
signed in February, 1848, ended the long war
between Mexico and the United States.

Windwagon Smith was one of the more original dreamers whose startling appearance on the streets of Westport was first described in the *Kansas Historical Quarterly*. Elaborating and embroidering, W. S. Campbell, writing under the pseudonym of Stanley Vestal, told the story of Smith in *The Santa Fe Trail*, calling him Windwagon "Thomas." Wilbur Schramm wrote a less fanciful version published by the *Atlantic Monthly* in 1941, but by then Windwagon Smith had passed into legend as well as history. Disney made him the focus of a thirty-minute animated cartoon; folklorists blurred him into a legend with the likes of Mike Fink and Paul Bunyan. For a typical example see *Tall Tale America,* by Walter Blair (Coward, McCann, 1944).

I've drawn on all these sources for the bones of this story as well as on such firsthand reports as Josiah Gregg's *Commerce of the Prairies* and reports of men on expeditions sponsored by the U.S. Army and Topographical Corps of Engineers, all of whom commented about the resemblance of the prairie to an ocean.

Eric Ericssen is my creation; undoubtedly there were many boys and girls in Westport whose wanderlust was aroused by the great wagon with its wind-filled sail. I invented Eric and stowed him below decks as the first windship built by the Overland Navigation Company made her maiden voyage outside Westport, Missouri.

Windwagon did depart town in true mythical fashion: as he had arrived. He was sighted once or twice thereafter, as the story relates. His final port remains unknown.

Was he con artist or dreamer? Both, in my opinion: a true dreamer cons himself first of all. In that respect, Windwagon ranks with Icarus, medieval alchemists, founders of utopian societies, or the men who searched for the Northwest Passage.

If Windwagon Smith sold the good citizens of Westport a wooden nutmeg, he was around when they discovered the spice was no more than a peg of cedar. A true hustler would have left town with the loot before deception was discovered. Windwagon remained, until the failure of his grand illusion. Going down with his ship in a dried mudhole, he went down to a place in history and folklore, thereby earning glory of a sort, in Eric Ericssen's eyes as well as our own.